OUTSIDE

THE

D1467303

Written by Arlene Lagos

Illustrated by Shawnee J. Lagos

OUTSIDE THE CIRCLE

Writer: Arlene Lagos

Editor: Elisabeth Kauffman

Illustrated by: Shawnee Lagos

Copyright © 2014 Arlene Lagos

ISBN-13: 978-1502997623

ISBN-10: 1502997622

First Edition: © 2014

DEDICATION

This story is dedicated to my daughter Shawnee, who helped me develop the characters, the story line and the overall theme. She is my inspiration and I'm proud to have had the opportunity to work with her on this project!

CONTENTS

Chapter One: Recess

Everyone's afraid of something. Things like spiders, snakes, clowns—even the dentist! My aunt is afraid of elevators and my Mimi doesn't like to drive. My mom told me it's normal to have fears. But, my fear doesn't FEEL normal. The one thing I fear above all creepy crawly things or things that go bump in the night is—recess.

Today's my second day of third grade and already everything is so different to me. Back in kindergarten it seemed like everyone was your friend. We all played together. In the first and second grade, I noticed that some people stopped playing in large groups and formed smaller ones. This year, it's even worse. Everyone seems to have a friend to play with but me! I had a best friend named Anna that I spent the first few years of school playing with, but she moved to New York over the summer.

I spent so much time with her that I didn't really know anyone else. So here I am, sitting in the classroom surrounded by kids, dreading what will happen in just a few minutes—recess. The rest of the school day doesn't bother me because everyone is too busy learning, so it feels like we are all together. But when recess comes around, that's when the staring and the whispering start. Watching the clock tick closer to noon, my hands begin to sweat and my forehead gets really hot.

Yesterday was torture—I sat far away from the playground, leaning against a tree with my head buried in a book. Today, I am hoping that someone, even just one person, will ask me to play. The sound of the bell ringing makes me jump out of my seat and I feel my legs fighting to stay still. Even my body resists running outside. While everyone is heading for the playground, I stand very still in the classroom, staring out the window, clenching my library book.

"Is everything okay, Emma?" asks Mrs. Daniels. Looking up at her with my best puppy dog eyes, I try to come up with a reason why I need to go to the nurse instead of to recess. But, I don't like to lie. My mom says that lying just creates more problems, so I try to stall. "Maybe I could just stay in here and read?" I ask. "It's beautiful out, why don't you go play with your friends?" She replies. Staring down at my feet, I try not to let the tears in my eyes fall, but they do anyway. "I don't have any friends."

Mrs. Daniels cocks her head to the side and gives me that sad face all teachers give when they feel bad for you. My cheeks fill with the flush red color of embarrassment and I walk away as fast as I can, find my way to my tree, and bury my head in my book. At least this way, not playing with someone appears like it is my choice instead of just my reality.

Chapter Two: The Circle

Yesterday was horrible. While sitting by my tree I noticed many people staring at me. The boys would point and stare, the girls just formed small groups and whispered and laughed. Positive they were laughing at me, I turned my back to the playground for the rest of recess so nobody could see me crying.

Sitting once again at my desk, same as yesterday, I stare at the clock in despair, praying for rain.

"I want to talk to you all about a new program we are implementing on the playground," says Mrs. Daniels.

Oh please, I hope she doesn't pair us up into some forced buddy system. That would be the worst thing they could do!

"In an effort to stop bullying in the school and help promote growing friendships, Principal Skinner and I have painted a happy face on the concrete near the front of the playground area."

Maybe I spoke too soon. How is a happy face going to help?

Everyone looks up with wrinkled eyebrows. What could a happy face have to do with bullying? "We call it the friendship circle. Many schools are implementing it, some with benches, some with trees. We decided a happy face was the best idea." This is getting interesting, I'm not sure where she is going with this idea, but something about it makes me sit on the edge of my seat and hang on every word she said.

"The point of the friendship circle is to help people find each other. Many of you play alone, and there's nothing wrong with that. But, if any of you are looking for someone to play with, all you have to do is step inside the friendship circle and that will be your way of letting others know you are looking for someone to play with." She smiles a big toothy smile, proud of this great idea she has come up with. This sounds great to me, too! Now all I have to do is wait for someone to stand in the circle and then I can go to them and start making friends! The rest of the classroom seems to have different opinions about it as they chat with their friends on the way out to recess. Like a kid who first hears the sound of an ice cream truck approaching, I can't wait to run outside and see this magnificent circle! As everyone heads outside, I slip quietly through the crowd, eager to catch a glimpse of this happy face that just might save my social life. As I approach it, I look around at the reaction of the other kids. But when they get to the circle they glance down at it quickly, walk around it, and then walk as far away from it as they can. This is strange. Why wouldn't anyone want to stand in the circle? Disappointed, I sit down by my favorite tree and let out a sigh. Maybe they just need a little time. Holding my book up in front of my face now so I can keep my eyes pinned on the circle, I watch and wait for someone, anyone, to step inside. Ten minutes pass and still, not one person.

This is frustrating! There are plenty of other kids just like me that don't play with anyone, how come they aren't standing in the circle?

Looking closely, I notice some of the more popular kids making fun of it now. What are they doing? Why would they do that?

Boys are pushing each other into the circle and laughing.

"Dustin's a loser, he needs a friend— someone come rescue him!"

Oh no! This is horrible! This wonderful idea is being turned into something bad! Now nobody is going to want to step in the circle for fear of being called a loser. Could this day get any worse? Just as the bell rings for us to come in, my question is answered. Walking near the circle, I hesitate for a moment to get a good look at the bright yellow face and welcoming smile. Suddenly, someone bumps into me, pushing me inside the circle and causing me to drop my book.

When I turn to see who it is, I realize
right away that it wasn't an accident.
It's Tina and her friends, also known as
"the blondes." They are always walking
around school like they own it. They
earned the nickname "the blondes"
because I swear you can't be friends
with them if your hair is any other color.
Looks like I won't have to worry about
that with my wavy brown hair. Not that
I would want to be friends with them
anyway. They are always making
remarks about people's clothes, or their

hair, or their weight. They even picked one this one girl last year for being short. The next day the girl came to school in high heel sneakers! She's been wearing them every day since.

Frustrated, I pick up my book. I may be shy and afraid to talk to people, but I am not afraid to give this mean girl and her mean friends the stink eye! They are still pointing and laughing when I purse my lips and squint my eyes, making sure my face is in perfect position as I walk out of the circle and towards them.

For a quick second, I see Tina hesitate, and then turn around and signal to her friends to walk away with her. Take that, blondie!

Chapter Three: The Contest

Finally the weekend is here and I can relax without fear of being whispered or pointed at. Almost every weekend, my dad brings me to the school park so I can play on the four-person seesaw. That's my favorite because it's the only thing still in good condition on the playground. But I never go on it during recess, mostly because the same people always get to it first, and then stay on it all through recess. Also, I don't go on it because I don't have any friends to play on it with anyway, so why bother?

But since it's the weekend and most

kids go to the other park, I get to play

on the school playground with my dad

without any worries of staring,

laughing, or pointing! Today my mom

and my Mimi came to the park with us

and I got them to all ride on the seesaw

with me! It was the first time there was

ever four of us and I was so excited! But

still, it would be nice if I had friends to

ride it with.

"This playground needs some work," Dad says.

It is very old. Everything except the four-person seesaw was rusting. The slide was almost always closed down for one reason or another.

"I was reading about a contest in one of my magazines the other day, something about how the winner gets a new playground donated to their school," Mom says.

Sitting up straight, my ears are perked as I listen closely.

"Really? What do you have to do to win?" I ask.

Mom holds up her finger signaling me to wait a moment and runs back to the car to get the magazine. My brain starts thinking of a million different things. Imagine all the friends I would make if I won the contest for the school! Everyone would want to hang out with me! Maybe they would let me help design it and I could put in four-person seesaws all over the playground so everyone would get a turn!

Jumping off the seesaw, I grab the magazine out of my mother's hands as soon as she reaches me and run off to my favorite tree to read about the contest. The contest rules state that each team has to come up with the best way to use no more than $100 to better the lives of senior citizens in their community. Team—that word keeps hitting me like a brick in the face. Reading the rules further I realize that each team has to be made up of at least four people in order to register. Ugh.

Maybe my family could help me?

Continuing to read the rules it clearly states that all team members have to be from the same school in order to qualify.

"Oh come on!" I yell out loud.

"Everything okay, Emma?" asks Dad.

Feeling defeated, I stand up and walk over to where my family is sitting and hand the magazine back to my mom with a sad, defeated look on my face.

"What's wrong Emma?" asks Mom.

Looking into my mom's peaceful eyes, I don't have the heart to tell her that I have no friends. Heat rushes to my face and before I know it, I can't hold it in any longer. Tears form and I press my head inside my mother's arms, letting out a loud cry, one that has been desperate to get out since school started. Trying to cheer me up, my father points out the happy face on the playground. "Hey Emma, is this the friendship circle the school sent a letter home about?" asks Dad.

My tears fall faster now, as I am embarrassed, angry, lonely, and sad. My father comes over and holds his arms out for a hug, but I just run back to my tree. No kid wants to tell their parents that they have no friends.

Is this what the rest of my life at school was going to feel like? If only someone would just stand inside that stupid circle, my life would be so much easier. As if reading my mind, my Mimi comes up beside me and sits down at a nearby bench.

"I read about the friendship circle, too. Have you thought about standing in it Emma?" she asks. A flood of horror fills inside my chest at the suggestion.

"Mimi, if I stand inside that circle, everyone will make fun of me for not having any friends." Holding her hand out to me, I grab it and she sits me down on the bench next to her, puts one arm around me and uses the sleeve from her other arm to wipe away my tears. "You know, Emma, when I was younger, I used to go out dancing with my girlfriends. Everyone would stand around the dance floor in a circle moving their hips to the music, but not daring to step out onto the floor.

It would take hours before people finally started dancing. This happened almost every time we went out and became very frustrating to me."

"How come they didn't dance?" I ask.

"They wanted to! But nobody wanted to be FIRST. Everyone was afraid, just like you are afraid. But I loved to dance and so one night, I got tired of waiting and I jumped onto that dance floor and started moving around like nobody was watching."

Mimi smiles as she lifts up her elbows, stands up a few inches off the bench, and wiggles her hips, which makes me laugh.

"What happened?"

"At first people laughed, but eventually, they all ended up on the dance floor! We had a ball, and everyone danced all night long and you know what's even funnier? None of my friends could remember who first started dancing!"

"Seriously?" I ask.

"Seriously," said Mimi.

"Emma, someone needs to have the courage to go first. Maybe, you could be that someone."

Mimi always gives the best advice.

She's right. The only way I am going to be able to even enter the contest is if I have a team of four.

That means I needed at least three friends.

That means I had to stand in the friendship circle.

The question is, will I find the courage to do it?

Chapter Four: Finding Courage

I decide I will do it on a Friday. That way, if it goes horribly wrong, I will have two days to let the gossip and humiliation die down before I have to face everyone again.

Today is Friday. Standing in my bedroom staring at myself in the mirror, I comb my wavy brown hair. My reflection peers back at me and I practice my brave face.

"Someone has to be first," I say out loud.

Straightening up my shoulders I take

one last look in the mirror, turn and grab

my backpack and head downstairs. I'm

almost out the front door when I hear

my mom yell from the kitchen.

"Don't forget breakfast!"

Too nervous too eat, I grab a banana

throw it in my coat pocket and head to

the bus stop.

"Good luck today Emma!" mom shouts.

But I am too nervous to reply. Somehow I'm afraid that if I open my mouth, all the courage will come spilling out of me.

As usual, I sit in the front seat of the bus so I don't have to walk by anyone. Cramming my bag between my ankles I stare out the window as the bus makes its way to the school.

The entire morning at school is a blur to me as all I can focus on is recess. Staring at the clock, I can almost hear the second hand tick-tick-tick away as if getting louder and louder. A drop of sweat falls onto my desk and I realize its coming from my forehead. Wiping it away with my sleeve I look back down and realize that I haven't even started the math quiz in front of me—it's completely blank.

"Five more minutes, class," said Mrs. Daniels.

Quickly, I pull out my pencil and answer as many problems as fast as I can. It's a good thing that math comes easily to me; the last thing I want is for Mrs. Daniels to keep me from going to recess so that I can finish this quiz! Two more problems to go, I can make it.

"Time's up, pencils down. Please pass your quizzes forward."

Phew! I don't know how well I did, but at least I finished, and without a second to spare. The bell rings and a lump forms in my throat—it's recess time.

As the doors swing open and children push past me, I walk slowly as if I'm stuck in a river of bubble gum trying to reach my destination. The only thing really holding me back is fear. All these voices in my head—like my mom and dad, and my Mimi—telling me, "You can do it, Emma!" are what's keeping me from turning around and running in the opposite direction.

I'm in such a daze at this point that I haven't even realized that at some point I had dropped my book and jacket on the ground. All I can think about is the circle. It's like a magnet taking hold of whatever courage I may have within me and drawing me in. Just a few steps away, I dare not look up to see who might be looking back. I hear a few snickers in the distance but I block them out by singing, "Go, Emma, go! Go, Emma, go!" in my head.

Taking a deep breath, I jump with both feet into the middle of the circle, close my eyes, place my fists on my hips and hold my head up high. I can feel people moving around me. I can hear their whispers, some laughing; I swear I can even feel them pointing. Footsteps approach and then walk away. Fear is now running through my body from head to toe and I fight the urge to cry—when suddenly, I feel a tapping on my shoulder.

Opening my eyes I look at the person

tapping me, then my jaw drops open.

"Hi, my name's Elisa," she says.

She looks at me for a response but I

can't speak. A small tear is fighting to

escape my eye as I stare at her in utter

disbelief. Then she smiles the biggest,

happiest smile.

"Do you want to play?" she asks.

In that moment, I feel the weight of the

world melt off my shoulders. A large

smile runs across my face as I let out a

deep sigh of relief.

"Yes. I would REALLY love that!" I say.

"What's your name?" she asks.

"My name is Emma."

"You are brave, Emma. My papa always tells me to have courage. He would like you."

She puts her hand out to me, and without hesitation, I put mine in hers. Together we walk out of the circle towards the grass and sit down. I've done it. I have made my very first friend.

Chapter Five: Brand New World

The day is over and I can't wait to tell my mom and dad about Elisa. The bus pulls up at my stop and I run down the stairs, jumping into the street as if it were going to explode I am so excited. As the bus pulls away I run toward my mother with the biggest smile on my face. She seems happy and confused at the same time as I leap into her arms and hug her as tight as I can.

"You sure are in a good mood!" she says.

She places me down on the ground and I tell her all about Elisa. How I had the courage to stand in the circle, how I made my first friend and how we played all through recess together.

"Good for you Emma! I'm so proud of you!" she says, hugging me and kissing my forehead.

"Elisa asked me if I could have a play date this weekend, maybe even a sleepover at her house. Can I, Mom? Can I please?" I beg.

"Why don't your father and I contact her parents and we can set up a time where we can meet them first, before we decide on a sleepover."

Suddenly, my mother's phone rings. From the look on her face, she doesn't recognize the number. I pray it is Elisa's mom. Knowing how our moms think, Elisa and I have come up with a plan to have her mom call my mom.

"We would love to come over for lunch tomorrow. That would be lovely. What's your address? Yes, I know where that is. Can we bring anything? Are you sure? Okay, we'll see you at Noon tomorrow, thank you." Mom hangs up.

"Elisa's parents have invited us for lunch, our whole family!" she says.

I can't wait. I am so excited. I'm pretty sure I won't sleep that night. I wonder what her house looks like, what her room looks like, and if she likes to read like I do. There is still so much I don't know about her. I know that her family can speak Spanish, and so can she. We will be eating all these dishes that I have never heard of before like arroz con leche and carne asada. Even my parents think it sounds like a great treat to try new foods and meet people that are from another country.

Walking into their home, I am amazed at how colorful the inside of their house is! Unlike our house that's full of lots of beige and pale yellows, they had a brick-red living room, and a bright orange kitchen filled with beautiful pictures like I have never seen before. We walk out to their back patio and there is an entire buffet of food before us. Rice and steak, beans, and chips and salsa! My mother brought her homemade potato salad because she believes no matter what, you should never show up empty handed. They seem to like it as much as we enjoy their food.

While our parents talk, Elisa shows me her room. It feels so good to have a friend again! It reminds me of my friend Anna that moved to NYC. I still missed her very much but I am happy to finally have made a new friend.

"I got this doll from my *Abuela*," Elisa says.

"What's an *Abuela*?" I ask.

"It's Spanish for grandmother."

"I call my grandmother Mimi. I think it's an Irish thing, but I'm not really sure." I say. We play for a while and Elisa shows me all her favorite things. She even teaches me a few words in Spanish like *hola*, which means hello; and *gracias*, which means thank you. We giggle as I practice rolling my r's when I said the word *perro*, which means dog; not to be confused with *pero* which means but.

Not the body part, although I keep saying it wrong on purpose because it's funny to say and doesn't feel like a bad word because it's in another language. Our giggling is interrupted by a knock on the door. Elisa's mom enters followed by mine.

"So I hear there're two girls in here dying to have a sleepover?"

Both our faces light up as we scream with glee and then run over and hug our mothers, then jump up and down in a circle.

That night, I tell Elisa about the contest.

About how badly we need a new

playground and how important it is to

me that we try to win. I am scared to ask

for her help, having known her for less

than 48 hours. But, to my surprise, she

is excited and wants to help.

"We are going to need to find at least

two more people," she says.

"Do you know anyone?" I ask.

"Not really. I just moved her over the summer and realized pretty quickly that everyone already made all the friends they wanted and it seemed as if they had no room for one more."

"I know the feeling."

"But I think if we both stand in the circle, perhaps more people will come. There are other kids out there just like us," says Elisa.

Oh man. It was hard enough standing in the circle the first time, now I have to do it again? She must have seen the look of horror on my face at the suggestion because suddenly she grabs my hand and squeezes it.

"We can do it together. It worked the first time, what do we have to lose?"

That night, I sleep better than any other night I can remember, even if we did stay up until eleven o'clock giggling. It's a brand new world, and I am living in it happily.

Chapter Six: Almost There

Monday comes around and my mind races as I wait again in anticipation of recess. At least this time, I have a friend who is willing to take the plunge into the dreaded circle by my side. The bell rings and everyone runs outside. Just as we planned, Elisa and I meet up at my favorite tree.

"Are you ready?" she asks.

"Yes…no… I'm scared."

"It will be fine. You did it once, you can do it again and this time, I'll be right beside you."

Elisa grabs my hand and we walk towards the circle and step inside. This time I keep my eyes open and look around at people's reactions. There isn't as much snickering as I thought there would be. There isn't as much laughter as I had heard when I first did it. For the most part, anyone looking just seems— stunned.

Out of the corner of my eye I see a girl stand up and take a few steps towards us and then stop. I remember her last year from gym class. Her name is Tolya. She always wears these really big sweatshirts, even when it's hot out. I think she is self-conscious about her size. She is taller and a bit heavier than the average third grader. But that kind of stuff doesn't bother me. We lock eyes and I smile at her and wave her over. A large smile stretches across her face and she walks toward the circle.

"Your name's Tolya, right?" I ask.

"Yes, hi," she says.

"My name is Emma and this is Elisa.

Do you want to play with us?"

"That would be cool."

While this is happening it looks as if

Elisa has recruited someone as well. But

not just any somebody; she recruited—a

blonde!

"This is Melissa. Melissa, this is Emma

and—"

"Tolya. This is Tolya," I say.

We all stare at each other. We are such an unlikely group, I wonder if it will work out. Will we all get along? Will they be interested in the contest? We all step out of the circle, find a patch of grass, and sit down. It seems for a while as if we just stare at one another. We are all so different. I am small and short, with brown hair and freckles. Elisa is a little thicker in the waist and has darker skin compared to my pasty white freckled skin; she has black curly hair, and a round face. Tolya is very tall and has the darkest skin I had ever seen. She also has these huge cheeks that I wanted to pinch so badly, but I don't want to freak her out. Melissa is even taller, wears glasses and has really short blonde hair. Most girls in our grade have long hair; it is interesting to see someone with such short hair. We take turns talking about our lives, our families, and where we come from. Elisa has moved the farthest, from Bogotá, Columbia in South America. Tolya's family moved to the suburbs from the city. Melissa has lived in our town since she was born, just like me.

"I don't remember you being in school before?" I say.

"I was home-schooled," says Melissa.

"What's that like?" Tolya asks.

"Well, the school part of it was okay; but I got really lonely and so when I went into remission, my parents promised I could go to public school," says Melissa.

"What's remission?" asks Tolya.

"I have cancer. Remission means that the treatment worked and I'm doing better. That's why my hair is starting to grow back; I used to be bald," Melissa says. "You were bald!" Elisa shouts. The three of us look at her with pity, but she just smiles. She opens up her backpack and pulls out some pictures from before the cancer when she had long curly blonde hair, and then during the cancer when she had none. She isn't looking for pity. It seems if anything, she is just happy to be alive.

As the three of them continue to share stories I remain silent, falling back into my own thoughts.

Here I am, worried about making friends, afraid to stand in a stupid circle, and this girl lost her hair! She had to be home-schooled and wasn't even able to be around kids! It makes me feel like my fears and insecurities are foolish. Something about Melissa makes me feel stronger. Looking at her smiling back at us, knowing what she had already battled by the age of eight—I envy her.

The bell rings and we exchange phone numbers quickly before running back into school. Having spent my entire recess with my new friends, I had forgotten to go to the bathroom. After much pleading, my teacher excuses me and I run there as fast as I can, forgetting that I could get in trouble for running in the halls. Luckily, nobody saw me.

While washing my hands in the bathroom, I hear someone crying in the stall behind me. I'm not really sure what to do; I have spent many a day crying in that same stall. Perhaps it's a newfound courage I have from making friends, but something makes me wad up some toilet paper and hand it under the door.

"Are you okay?" I ask.

"I'm fine, thank you."

I recognize the voice; it's Tolya!

"Tolya, it's Emma. Do you want to talk?"

Suddenly, the door opens and Tolya stares at me with big teary eyes and a wad of tissue in her hands.

"Oh my goodness, what happened?" I ask.

"I'm just so happy," she says.

"You are crying because you are happy?"

Tolya steps out of the stall, tossing her used tissues in the garbage. She walks over to the sink and begins washing her hands and cleaning up her face.

"Do you know how hard it is for someone like me to make friends?" she asks.

"What do you mean, someone like you?" I ask. "Emma, I'm the ONLY black person in the entire school."

"Oh. Yeah. I guess that would be kind of hard." The thought had never crossed my mind. I have seen her around school, but she always seemed to want to be alone. Maybe she doesn't after all. Maybe she is just like me, hoping to make a friend, but too scared to try.

"Well Tolya, you could be purple, and it wouldn't matter to me, because you are my new friend," I say.

Tolya and I hug and giggle as we fix our hair and blow kisses to ourselves in the mirror.

Once again I realize that I am not the only person that had it tough making new friends. Maybe standing in that circle isn't just about me anymore. Maybe it isn't even about the contest. I did something that changed other people's lives.

"Thank you Emma," says Tolya.

"I'll call you tonight, friend!" I say,

running out of the bathroom.

Chapter Seven: The Project

A week has passed since my new friends arrived in my life. During that week, we spent every recess together hanging out on our patch of grass and sharing stories of our hopes and dreams. The more we talked, the more I realized that even though we looked so different on the outside, we were very much alike on the inside. I decided that today I would bring up the contest.

Pulling out the magazine, I read the article out loud. They listen to every word I read. Then, I put the magazine down and wait for a reaction, praying that it is a good one. Elisa, who already knows about the project, speaks first.

"I think we would make a great team. What do you girls think?"

Tolya and Melissa look at each other and then back at us. My heart is beating so fast.

"So if we win, the school gets a new playground?" asks Tolya.

"Yes. What do you think?" I say.

Suddenly, Tolya lunges at me and tackles me with the biggest hug I have ever received. Melissa jumps up and starts shouting with joy. I'm guessing they are just as excited as Elisa and I about the contest! Before I know it, we are all dancing without music on our small patch of grass without a care in the world about who might be watching.

That weekend, my parents invite the girls over for a sleepover, all three of them! My mother has tea with the other moms in our kitchen as us girls settle in. I guess parents have a thing about getting to know each other. Elisa's mom brought us "food for thinking", while Tolya's mom who is a lawyer, went through all the rules of the contest and wrote them down in a way that we kids could understand, highlighting very specific things to make sure we couldn't be disqualified. Melissa's mom has done her share of fundraising when Melissa was sick in order to pay for her medical bills, so she brought over information about different charities. But they leave the idea for the project to us.

"So we have to come up with a way to better the life of Senior Citizens in our town with no more than $100. We can't use the money to raise more money and we can spend less than $100 but not a penny more," says Tolya.

She reminds me of her mom, standing tall and proud when she speaks. It's amazing how much confidence she has in this moment, compared to how shy she was when we first met. In fact, I notice that all of us seem more outgoing. I guess having friends brings out an inner strength in people.

"What if we made them all friendship bracelets?" Elisa suggests.

"That will take too long. What about a pet for the senior center, like a mascot?" says Melissa.

"The rules state that the project can't accrue additional costs," says Tolya. "What does that mean?" I ask. "It means that once they get a pet, it's going to cost more money to feed it and take care of it and that would exceed the $100 over time," says Tolya. We come up with ideas all night, and many of them are great, but they aren't unique. We need something powerful, something that nobody else has thought of.

We pour over the list of charity ideas and come up empty-handed. None of us had realized how little $100 really is in the adult world. It really doesn't buy much. We have hit a wall and it is getting late.

The next morning we head downstairs for breakfast. My dad has cooked up a hot batch of blueberry pancakes.

Everyone is quiet; perhaps because we have exhausted every inch of our brains the night before trying to come up with ideas.

"Have you girls come up with anything yet?" asks Dad.

"Not yet. We kind of don't know what to do next," I say.

Dad looks at us. We are a sad bunch. We don't want to give up, but time is not on our side. We only have a week left before the submission deadline.

"My father used to tell me, if you have a problem that needs fixing, go to the source," Dad says.

Go to the source. What does that mean?

Go to the heads of the contest? I am

confused and barely able to finish my

pancakes.

"You mean like, talk to senior citizens?"

says Melissa.

Suddenly, a light goes on in my head

and I understand what my dad is

suggesting.

"We should go to the senior center

today in town and visit my Mimi! We

can talk to her friends and find out what

they need!"

Smiles grow back instantly on the faces of my friends as we all realize that this is by far, our best idea yet. Shoveling our breakfast as fast as we can into our mouths, we rush upstairs to get dressed.

Chapter Eight: The Senior Center

While my friends spend time in the recreational area speaking with some of the seniors, I sit with my Mimi and ask her as many questions as I can. "What kind of things do you like to do? What makes you happy Mimi?" I ask. "Oh I don't know. I guess I just like to relax and be with my friends," she says. As I continue to look around the center and listen to my Mimi talk, I try to find something that will spark an idea but nothing comes to me.

My mom stops by to see how we are doing.

"Hey there beautiful! Tonight's your lucky night, I can feel it!" says my mom. This is something she always says to my Mimi on Sundays, before Mimi heads to bingo.

"I'm not going tonight," says Mimi. My mother's jaw drops to the floor as does mine. Mimi ALWAYS goes to bingo. It's her favorite thing in the entire world!

"Are you sick Mimi?" I ask.

"No, not sick," she says. "None of my friends from the center go anymore on account of how dark it gets at night. We are getting older and our eyes just aren't what they used to be. You see Emma, there's no real light between the bus stop and the senior center. None of us can see very well at night after bingo, so we've just stopped going."

"We could drive you and your friends," my mother offers.

But Mimi just shakes her head. She is a very independent woman, which according to my mom, just means stubborn.

If she can't do it herself, she feels it isn't worth doing.

It makes me sad to think that my Mimi had to stop doing what she loves because of this. That's when it hits me—we could find a way to make it light enough for the seniors to take the bus to Bingo and get home safely!

"We are going to help you Mimi!" I yell, then kiss her on the cheek and run off to find my friends. Gathered back at my mom's house, the four of us begin coming up with ideas on how we can afford to light the area from the bus station to the senior center with no more than $100. "We can't raise money for a street light, and it costs way more than $100 for one of those. Plus, we'd have to get it up within the week. Plus, we would need more than one street light to cover the distance," says Melissa.

My mind is spinning out of control with ideas. Each idea gets rejected one after another. If Melissa says 'plus' one more time, I may just burst into tears.

"What if we bought them all flashlights?" says Elisa.

That's a great idea! If we go to the dollar store, we could get 100 flashlights. That way they would all have one! Elisa and I are smiling ear to ear, but Melissa looks on with a frown.

"I don't think that's going to work," she says.

I can't understand why not. When I need to see in the dark, I use a flashlight. This is a great solution!

"A lot of older people have arthritis and can't hold a flashlight. Many of them have walkers or canes," Melissa says.

This is true. My Mimi has trouble with her hands a lot.

"What if we made flashlight necklaces so they wouldn't have to hold them?" says Tolya.

Another brilliant idea! We are really getting somewhere now!

But then I remember that thing in the rules that Tolya had mentioned before about accrued cost. Then I think about batteries.

"Would batteries be an accrued cost?" I ask.

"Maybe. We should call the contest people and ask them." Says Tolya. "We don't want to submit this, then find out that we didn't follow the rules."

The next morning, I call the number on the magazine and wait patiently on speakerphone with my parents by my side for someone to answer. After being put on hold for three minutes, someone finally answers. I describe in detail our proposed project; the woman on the phone seems genuinely excited about our idea. Then I bring up the question about the batteries and she goes silent.

"I'm not one of the judges for the contest, but in my honest opinion, since that is such a gray area, I would advise that you rethink your contest entry," she says.

She hangs up the phone and I let out a sigh. Then I ask my mom what she means by 'gray area.' Mom replies that it means it may or may not disqualify you depending on the judges.

This is a chance we can't take. Sadness fills me and I need some fresh air.

Pedaling my bike through the neighborhood, I try to look for an answer. There is so little I knew at my age. There are so many rules. But, as my Mimi says, "If it was that easy to win a playground, everyone would do it." Turning the corner onto my street, I see my neighbor Mrs. Harrington working in her flower garden. She has the most beautiful flower garden on the entire street. Maybe even in the entire town!

She works on it everyday and I always enjoy looking at it from my bedroom window.

Smelling the sweet scents coming off the flowers, I am drawn in. I get off my bike, sit down next to Mrs. Harrington, and admire her flowers.

"How are you today Emma?" she asks.

"I'm okay. Just a little tired," I say.

She hands me a shovel and recruits me into helping her plant flowers. The colors and the scents instantly make me happy.

"Flowers would be nice for the Senior Center," I mumble to myself.

"What's that dear?" she says.

"Nothing. I'm just thinking out loud."

Pointing in the corner where I was to dig the next hole, I spot something odd in her flower garden. It is stuck into the ground, hidden. It seems like an odd thing to be placed in the middle of these beautiful flowers.

"What is this?" I ask.

"Oh, those are my solar lights."

"Solar lights?"

"You know how you can see my garden at night?"

"Yes, its lovely all lit up!" I say.

"That's what lights them up."

"They must have really small batteries," I say.

"They run on solar energy, Emma," she says. "That means from the sun. You see, during the day, they soak up the sun and store all the energy into a cell inside the top of the stake, and then when the sun goes down, they light up."

This is fascinating. Light from the sun…Light from the sun means no accrued cost! The sun is free!

"How much do they cost?" I ask.

"It depends on what size you get, but I just get the little ones for a dollar to hide behind the flowers."

My eyes light up. Can it be possible that I have found the solution to our problem?

"Can I borrow this? I'll bring it back I promise!" I ask.

Mrs. Harrington gives a nod and before she can even wave goodbye I am on my bike pedaling back to my house as fast as my little legs can go.

Chapter Nine: Light Up The Night

The distance from the bus stop to the Senior Center is the first thing we need to measure. Melissa's mom gives us a pedometer, which is a little device that measures distance and all sorts of other cool stuff!

It shows us how many steps we have taken, how fast we are going, how long it takes us to get there and how far we went! It even tells us how many calories we burned!

"It says we've walked 528 feet," says Elisa.

"How far is that in miles?" I ask.

"One-tenth of a mile," says Elisa.

"How long have we been walking for?" asks Tolya.

"For about a two and a half minutes," says Elisa.

After we record our information, we go back to my house so we can figure out what we need. Mrs. Harrington lets us borrow a few of her solar lights so we can space them out.

Elisa moves them around after the sun sets and we discover that placing the lights any more than 6 feet apart will start to make them too dim. Time to do some math.

"If we divide 528 feet by six feet, we'll see how many lights we need to buy," says Tolya.

"According to my calculations, we would only need to buy 88 solar lights to line the sidewalk from the Senior Center to the bus stop," says Melissa.

That is a great number! Mrs. Harrington told me that these lights could be purchased for as little as one dollar each, so if we only need 88, then we'll be under the $100 mark!

Off to the dollar store we go. My mom suggests we call ahead to make sure they have enough, so Melissa calls and they put them aside for us.

When the lady at the dollar store finds out what we were using them for, she offers to sell them to us for half price!

"I'm sorry we can't. The rules state, no charity," says Tolya.

We can't be certain if this is another 'grey area' but it isn't worth taking the chance.

"Good thinking, Tolya," says Elisa.

The next day is Sunday and we are ready to line the sidewalk! Our submission has to be mailed in by no later than that Wednesday, so we are really pushing our deadline.

As the four of us line the sidewalks, we hear clapping and cheering coming towards us. My Mimi is leading a Senior Center rally right to us to support our cause!

Elisa's mom takes out her camera and photos us putting the lights in, surrounded by the seniors cheering us on. This is going to be a great submission!

As I look around me, I feel so proud of what we have accomplished. Because of our courage to stand in the circle, we have become a team, and we are making my Mimi and her friends very happy. It doesn't even matter if we win the contest at this point. We have won something much bigger than that. We helped our community. We really did make the lives of our Senior Citizens better!

Even though we have school the next day, our parents let us stay up until dark, so we can see the lights for the first time and wave the seniors off to Bingo. Standing at the senior center, we are amazed that almost all the seniors who can walk take the bus from the center to the bingo hall. We walk alongside them and as the sun begins to set, we can see the lights from the solar stakes begin to shine. We can't wait for them to get back and see if it will be bright enough for the walk home.

As the bus pulls up, my Mimi is the first one off. They get off the bus one by one, and as they do, more and more spectators gather around us, watching. It is as if the entire town is out there cheering us on! The sidewalk is so bright and everyone comments on how much better they can see with the new solar lights in place.

"You girls did a great thing here," says Mimi.

The next day after school, we gather together at Melissa's house and we each submit an essay about our project. We also include the pictures Elisa's Mom took, as well as some letters that the seniors have written on our behalf about their experience.

Hand-in-hand we walk to the end of Melissa's driveway and put our contest entry into the mailbox. All we can do now is wait.

Chapter Ten: The Results

It has been two months since we mailed in the submission. At first it was all we could talk about, but as time dragged on, it made us anxious and miserable. We made a pact not to talk about it anymore. Days passed by and we played on our patch of grass during recess. It was the happiest two months of my life. Now sitting in our area, watching the other kids playing nearby, something catches my eye.

Jared Baker is standing in the circle!

Jared Baker is one of the most popular

boys in our grade! Pointing but unable

to speak, my friends look over as well

with jaws dropped open wide. He is

holding a football in his hand high

above his head. Listening closely, I hear

him yell.

"Who wants to play touch football?"

At least ten boys on the playground stop whatever is distracting them and run to the circle toward Jared. Then they all run off toward the field to play. Looking back, I see two more kids standing in the circle, trying to get a game of Frisbee going. A few others join them.

"It's working. People are using the circle!" I say.

"You made it cool, Emma," says Elisa.

My mind is spinning. I haven't paid much attention to anything outside of my new friends in months. I had no idea people were actually using the circle! Suddenly, the outside speaker turns on.

"Emma Reilly, Melissa Harris, Elisa Hernandez and Tolya Johnson, please report to the principal's office."

I've never been called to the principal's office in my life. Instantly I am filled with fear.

"Do you think we are in trouble?" I ask.

"Maybe it's about the contest," says Tolya.

Grabbing our stuff as fast as we can, we run towards the office, eager with anticipation.

"Please come in, ladies," says Principal Skinner.

He is sitting at his desk with Mrs. Daniels standing behind him. My hands are shaking and I can feel my face getting hot. Elisa is fidgeting and Tolya is biting her nails. Melissa seems calm and attentive. At least one of us is calm.

"We received a letter telling us that four of our students had won us a free playground. Do you know anything about this?"

Immediately, I jump out of my chair and throw my arms up in the air. "Yes! Yes! Yes!" I shout.

The other girls join me as we jump around in a circle and giggle at our success.

"They are writing an article in the town newspaper about what you girls did," says Mrs. Daniels. "This is very impressive, it's quite an accomplishment!"

"Yes, it is," says Principal Skinner. "And we are overwhelmed at how hard you worked on this project. The four of you are a dynamic team. Well done girls."

Later that afternoon after school gets out, we meet with the newspaper lady who listens to us tell our story about how it all started. We tell her about the friendship circle, how we all met, about the rules and the different ideas we had come up with and why we couldn't use them. We talk about my Mimi and the other seniors and show her the pictures. Then her photographer takes a picture of the four of us.

We decide to celebrate that weekend in the park with all of our families. We have a huge picnic and I get to taste lots of different foods and meet some of my friends' aunts, uncles, and cousins. The article comes out in the paper and I read it a hundred times.

Sitting on the picnic blanket eating my sandwich, I look at Elisa whose jaw is dropped and she is staring past me. I look over my shoulder to see what she is looking at and it's—Jared Baker!

He sits down next to me. Quickly, I shut my mouth and hope I haven't spilled any crumbs on my shirt. Swallowing the last piece of my sandwich I manage to get out a quiet, "Hi."

"I read your article in the newspaper," says Jared. "I can't believe you girls won us a new playground. We really needed it."

"You're welcome—I mean thanks— what I meant was—" My mind is blank. Talking to boys is not easy for me. But changing the subject is.

"I saw you in the circle the other day," I say. "Yeah, I love that thing now. It was always so hard to get all my friends together to play ball, I would find one and then lose another. Now with the circle, it's like a beacon, they see me standing there and I'm able to get them to stop what they are doing and pay attention for a minute." "That's a great idea. Boys have short attention spans," I say. Then I realize I probably just insulted him. I put my head down and blush a bit.

"No, you are right, we do," he says.

"But thanks to you, that's not so much of a problem. See you around Emma."

Thanks to me? Jared Baker just thanked me! Looking over at my friends they just stare at me as I stare back. He is definitely one of those extra cute boys that makes us all speechless.

Suddenly, Tolya bursts into uncontrollable laughter. Breaking our stare, we join her and the four of us roll around the picnic blanket laughing for what feels like forever.

Chapter Eleven: Emma

Today is the first day of fourth grade. The new playground has been installed over the summer. We came to visit it every week to take pictures of its progress. We even received calls from the contest folks asking us what we wanted most. We all answered pretty much the same thing, "At least two more of the four-person seesaws!"

The bell rings and the entire school is let outside for the opening ceremony. The four of us get to hold the giant scissors and cut the ribbon to officially open the playground. Mrs. Daniels makes sure we were the first ones to step foot on the playground and, of course, the four of us run to one of the new seesaws.

It is beautiful. Brand new bright green monkey bars, several cool slides with different heights, a rock wall, a balance beam, and three four-person seesaws!

As we sway up and down I think about where I was a year ago- the sad and lonely kid with no friends, hiding behind a book with my back against the tree. The circle saved me. Looking over at it in deep thought, I notice writing underneath it. Squinting my eyes to see if I can read it, I realize I needed to get closer so I jumped off the seesaw and head over to the circle.

I look down on the ground beneath my feet at the happy face. Written underneath it are the words 'The Friendship Circle', and written in tiny letters beneath that is a dash with the name "Emma". Quickly I look around and see Mrs. Daniels looking back at me. She winks at me, smiles, and walks back into the school.

The End

Made in the USA
Middletown, DE
27 November 2014